D1472165

MY MOTHER'S HANDS

WRITTEN BY SHEILA McGRAW & PAUL CLINE
ILLUSTRATED BY SHEILA McGRAW

A PETER SMITH BOOK FOR MEDLICOTT PRESS

Copyright © 1991 Sheila McGraw and Paul Cline for the text.
Copyright © 1991 Sheila McGraw for the illustrations.

All rights reserved. No part of this publication may be reproduced or
transmitted in any form or by any means, electronic or mechanical, including
photocopy, recording, or any information storage and retrieval system, without the
written consent of the publisher, except for purposes of review.

Library of Congress Number
90-063348

ISBN 0-9625261-2-6

A Medlicott Press Book
Distributed by Green Tiger Press,
Simon and Schuster Building.
1230 Avenue of the Americas
New York, New York 10020

Edited by Sarah Swartz, The Editorial Centre, Toronto.
Designed by Sheila McGraw
Typeset by Satellite Compositors, Toronto.

Manufactured in
Hong Kong

For Rosa Edith Medlicott Smith
— P.C.

For Caroline Elizabeth McGraw
— S.Mc.

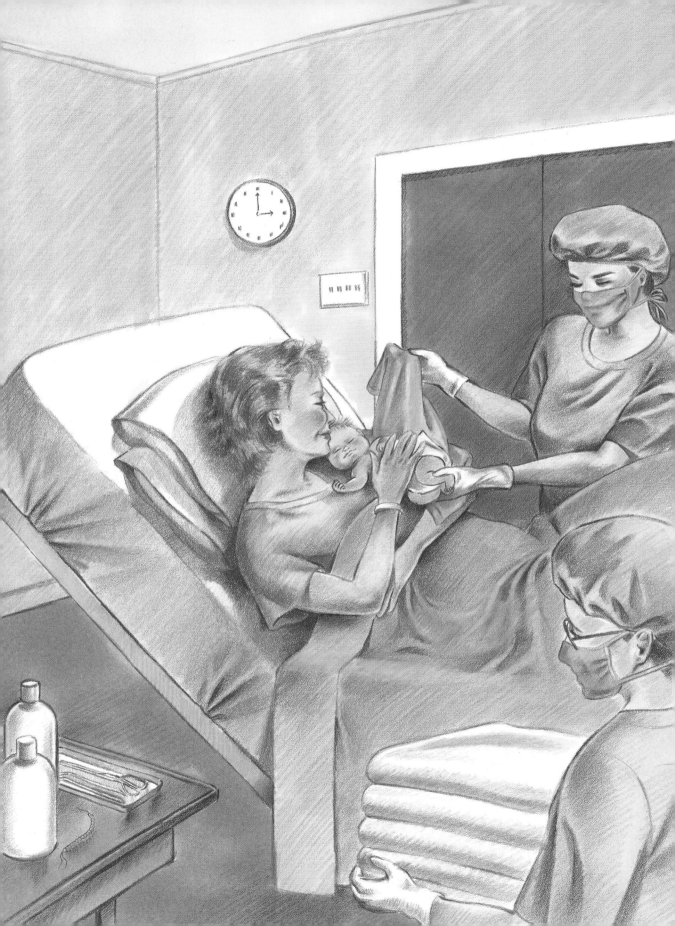

M
y mother's hands
are always there.

T
hey touch me,
hold me,
care for me.

When I was new, my mother
did everything for me. She fed me, bathed
and powdered me. She held me close to comfort me.
She counted my piggies and my fingers, told me rhymes
and stroked my cheek
with her fingertips.

My mother
dressed me up
and took me out
for everyone to see.
People looked at me
in my big baby carriage.
They made funny noises and silly faces
and rattled my toys to see me smile.

My mother's hands
keep me safe from harm.

They watch over me
through the night and day.

As I grew, I got more curious and more noisy.

No! and *Why?* were my favorite words.

I learned how to walk and then how to run.

I ran around and climbed up and fell down a lot.

My mother moved
all her nice things
very high-up,
out of my reach.
She said
that sometimes
just watching me
made her feel tired.

She played lots of games with me
like peek-a-boo and pat-a-cake.
I played games with her – the noisy-pot-banging game
and the mom-picks-up-the-toys game.

My mother's hands
are generous and kind.

They show me how to give.

Soon I was big enough to go to school.

My mother held my hand and walked with me every day.

For my birthday, I got a bicycle with streamers.

It had training wheels to keep me from tipping over.

I rode up-and-down

and up-and-down

and up-and-down

the sidewalk with Polly,

my favorite doll,

in the basket.

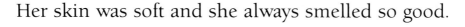

When I was all tired out,

my mother would hold me close.

Her skin was soft and she always smelled so good.

I learned how to count to ten and to dress myself.

I could climb on my stool to brush my teeth

and wash my hands and look in the mirror.

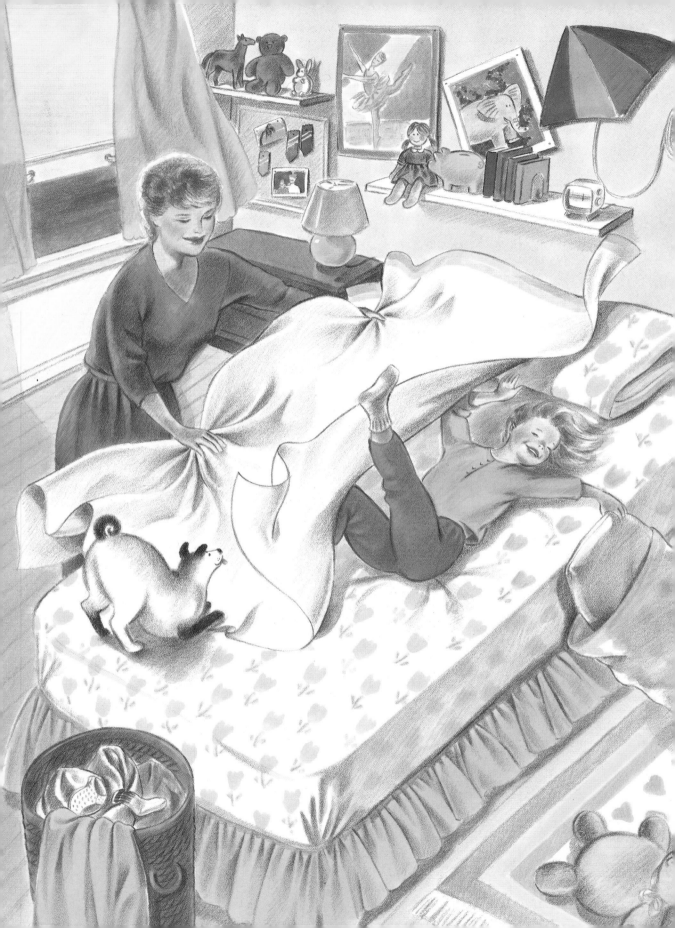

My mother's hands
are clever and busy.

They let me be part
of her world.

I grew taller and taller. I grew out of my clothes and wore out my shoes. Soon I was up to my mother's shoulder.

I could climb the apple tree in the Richardsons' backyard and pitch a no-hitter if I tried really hard. When my cousin got married, we went to her wedding. My mother bought me a new dress. When she saw me all dressed up, she said that she'd almost forgotten the pretty girl who was living inside me.

My mother always let me help in the garden. I planted seeds and picked ripe strawberries that were warm from the sun. She said that my thumbs were as green as hers.

My mother's hands
can do anything.

They are gentle and strong
at the same time.

Soon my body was changing and I began to wear
     grown-up clothes. My best friend Jenny came over
almost every night. We would do our homework,
     turn on the radio, lie on my bed, hug my teddy bears
and talk about school and boys.
  My mother called us
     the giggle girls.

  I helped
     my mother
  around the house.
Sometimes I made dinner
     or baked cookies all by myself. I loved to rest my
          head on her smooth lap. She would brush my hair
               and we'd talk about so many things.
     My mother said that I was big and little at the same time.

My mother's hands
hold inspiration.

They help me,
support me,
guide me.

In high school, I fell in love with Danny and
he fell in love with me. I had a part-time job at the
grocery store and I belonged to the theater group
at school. I even learned how to drive a car.

I was very busy.
There was so much
to think about
and so many
choices to make.
It was exciting
and scary
at the same time.

Whenever Danny and I went out on a date,
my mother said don't be late; I always was.
I said don't wait up; she always did.

My mother's hands hold me
even as they let me go.